When Fiction and Withheld Truths Say A Lot

MICHAEL NENO

When Fiction and Withheld Truths Say A Lot

Michael Neno

WORKBOOK PRESS LLC
187 E Warm Springs Rd,
Suite B285, Las Vegas, NV 89119, USA

Website: https://workbookpress.com/
Hotline: 1-888-818-4856
Email: admin@workbookpress.com

Ordering Information:
Quantity sales. Special discounts are available on quantity purchases by corporations, associations, and others. For details, contact the publisher at the address above.

ISBN-13:   978-1-955459-35-8 (Paperback Version)
                978-1-955459-36-5 (Digital Version)

REV. DATE: 04.05.21

Acknowledgement

This is a way of acknowledging those who have helped me along the way.

To my loving wife Michelle, I owe you a lot since the beginning until now.

To my family and friends, you've been a big help.

Telling my story has allowed me to reflect on how far I've come to inspire more people to look always at the brighter side of life.

And also the fact that I have been supported by the very best, to whom I can only say a truly heartfelt thank you.

Contents

Chapter 1 10

Chapter 2 19

Chapter 3 33

Chapter 4 44

Chapter 5 52

Chapter 6 61

Author's Gallery Over the Years 73

Chapter 1

In the year 1964, in the county of Devon in England, a married mother with two children, left her family for unknown reasons. Only to return a year later with another baby, (me) who she had tried to get rid of before my birth thankfully without success, only to have another child before disappearing again when I was aged only two years old.

Even treated exactly the same as my other half siblings, I knew somehow inside of me that I was different to them owing largely to my having thick curly bright ginger hair compared to the jet black colour of the rest of the family.

All through the first thirteen years of my childhood, my family life was a good and happy. Despite my private feelings regarding my parenthood, even with the three new siblings and a new mum after my dad remarried. All that begun to change when on my 13th birthday he informed me that he was not my biological father which I had always known inside with my family also becoming aware of it.

For myself, this news was quickly spread around including with my school friends with quite different responses. For most I was the same person but unfortunately for others mainly my new mum and step siblings I felt unwanted and a disliked inconvenience to their own wants.

Without playing on it I lived on usual trying my best to please others more and more often at my own cost. I finished my schooling with worse exam results owing largely to my own fault, because aged nine I was prescribed glasses which because of their thick glass look. I had carried them in my pocket due to personal vanity hence my not being able to see the classroom blackboard.

With lesser than wanted results I had to take any kind of work that I could just to pay the justly wanted keep asked for by my parents ending up picking fresh fruit and veg for up to twelve hours a day seven days of the week which to be honest I really enjoyed for a few months despite the low pay.

By the time that I was seventeen I acquired a part time job in a supermarket about three miles away from home which I almost instantly was accepted in by everyone there. An old small market town with its own 14th century clock tower and open air farmers market.

It was then that on returning home after finishing work at eight pm on a dark dry night in November that on reaching the brow of a hill walking up to the small village where I lived that up above me in the chilly sky I saw blocking out the star light was a massive triangular shaped craft motionless hovering with no sounds at all.

This was in no way any kind of man-made machine meaning it must be from another world which held my gaze transfixed on it for about five minutes until a beam of bright light came down passing over the ground as if it was a search light searching for something slowly passing right over me before going out and the craft suddenly shot straight up and disappeared.

Unaffected yet quite amazed other than a slight tingling sensation through my whole body briefly I just continued home arriving about an hour later than normal but saying nothing of my experience because I was all too aware of the way that those in power ridicule, lie and even destroy anyone who speaks out to keep their own control of lives.

The next day a Friday as I went about my usual every day routine of serving the customers at work while quietly thinking about the previous night's happenings without paying too much attention to them things would start to change very soon for me.

It was whilst serving on the stores fresh meats and cheeses counter that a very attractive young woman amongst those waiting for service allowed another a person to go before her so that I would be the next to serve her. As she stepped closer to my counter ready for serving I asked what I could get for her trying not to be affected by her very good looks with a hair style looking like an ancient Egyptian princess with a perfect shaped body in a five feet 9-inch-high frame but more over her wishes as a customer.

As I looked at her face without moving her lips I heard clearly in my head her asking what I liked to eat and filled her order handing it over to her. She raised her gloved hand thanking me saying, "See you later" and took it before again without moving her lips thanked me saying "until later" and left.

About thirty minutes later, I was leaving work and heading home again under a thick cloud but still feeling chilly out of the town and onto the hedged rural lane toward my home remembering the previous night's happenings still not considering anything else. That is until approaching the brow of the hill close to home when ahead of me I could just make out the shape of a person seemingly waiting for something or one hopefully me causing me to hope it was the woman who I had earlier served.

You can imagine my surprise when I was close enough to see if it was there was a screech of tyres as a dark car stopped and two men wearing black grabbed at the woman and tried pulling her into their car as she tried to fight back. I broke into a sprint just grabbing her arm as one of the men tried to push me back.

Luckily I managed to push my way between them telling the woman to run as I stopped her attackers by swinging fists and punching as she became free of them. Suddenly there was a really bright flash of light behind me and then the attackers clambered back into their car and sped off back toward the town. With that immediate threat over I turned back toward the woman only to see no sign of her.

Once home I telephoned the local police and informed them of what had just happened before noticing that during our scuffling I had been cut on my lower left arm and across what felt like my back. I described as best I could the attackers, car used and a description of the woman.

After sharing my story with the police officer who had quickly arrived after I had returned to the spot. After informing him of that I knew I started to turn in order to continue home when the officer grabbed my arm saying "You need to go to hospital and have your wounds seen to," before getting onto his walkie talkie and asking for an ambulance to be sent. Once at the hospital the emergency doctor in the presence of the officer said that there was no way that the wound on my back could possibly be self-inflicted supporting my claim. Plus, if the cut had been a millimetre or two deeper I may have died so I should not try to move much for a couple of days.

Unknown to me the police released the news to the media hoping for more information. This in turn triggered an onslaught of press and media calls wanting interviews which I declined due to the missing woman who I had in a way saved and with the adrenaline that had kept me going returning to its normal level pain was being felt much more.

You can imagine my surprise when getting home again about 2 am I unlocked my door and on walking back in I was faced by the woman that had vanished just standing there before me. As before without moving her lips she said, "Hello Michael my name is Karolla and I needed to see you again. You have risked your life to save mine earlier and I have a duty to serve you in any way to repay you for my life." I was so shocked that I needed to sit down to steady myself on hearing this before saying anything.

Wearing what looked like a pale white coloured one piece metallic looking jump suit made of an unknown material with a hooked cross insignia on the left hand upper chest an insignia that I had only ever seen on a TV program before relating to a symbol by the ancient Knights Templar. Being very tired and ever so confused I carefully sat down on my couch, "Please forgive me if I fall asleep Karolla, I must talk with you more when I am more with it. There is so much that I need to know so make yourself at home if you want to and I'll give you my full attention in a while."

With that I obviously fell asleep because when I opened my eyes again it was Sunday afternoon Had I just slept for over 24 hours.

With one eye closed I scanned around the room getting look at any surprise changes that may be there but all was okay and so I threw back the blanket that covered me to find out that I had been undress whilst asleep and not only that but the wounds I had suffered were fully healed without any sign of ever being there. What had happened to me, had I only dreamt it all and what about Karolla was she just in my mind?

I had no idea until picking up my coat from the floor I saw the blood stained rips in it, that told me that all this was not a dream after all but what about her, was she real and was she here when I got home. I remember thinking to myself that if she is real how can I see her again because without knowing it I was starting to love her but not in a romantic way, I just felt a need to be with her.

All began to make sense to me when suddenly the whole

room was lit up by a blinding flash of light and there were two figures, Karolla and an older man dressed in the same material as before. I should have been scared to death but lord knows why but I was quite calm, almost as if it was normal. With the two of them taking seats at my kitchen table the man introduced himself as her called Orsat, her father.

He also said, "We know that you almost paid the ultimate price to save my unknown to you my daughter. You have earned the highest honour to our people and I am willing to give you both my blessing as a married couple, but firstly are you ready to know everything. "Freezing in his place he turned his head toward his daughter and said "They are close. We must go again to keep him safe." and then shaking my hand the two of them vanished again.

Hearing the sound of walking coming up the gravel slope outside toward my door I just knew that it was who Orsat mentioned so quickly I moved the chairs around my kitchen table and wiped over the seats removing any sign of any one being there just in time for knocking at the door. On opening it I was met by two men dressed in black asking questions about the last few nights and the lady who I had saved.

Knowing that they were not from the police I played dumb asking them the sort of things that an uninformed person may ask. This I hoped would make them think that I knew nothing more and would leave again which they did or so I thought.

It was now the Monday morning and as normal I after preparing myself ready to go to work had a last quick ensuring there was no lights or unneeded electrical things left switched on before locking my door and going down the pathway toward the public pathway beside the road.

I looked both ways as one should always do before starting my walk into the town and to work feeling quite contented with Orsats surprise blessing on his daughters wanting to be my wife while questioning why she would even think of doing such a thing. Everything was so like a dream for me that I failed to notice a dark green saloon car with blackened windows gently pull out behind keeping a safe from distance me.

Once I had walked onto the road leading away from my home village and along the part with high hedges the following car sped forward purposely just missing me making me almost fall into the hedge. This I believe was intended on being somewhat of a warning that my life was now in danger from parties' unknown for reasons that I did not as yet fully know or understand. How could I with nobody to talk to? As it was I continued to walk constantly aware and afraid.

It was whilst I was off the shop floor unpacking a new delivery of stock that I saw that one of the sealed packets had been opened and resealed again and on the top of it was drawn a hooked cross mark and I automatically knew it was meant for me and so I carefully opened it.

Inside was a circular solid gold medallion about two inches across with a star shaped sapphire set in which as I touched it shown out an image of Karolla saying "You are in danger from your leaders. They want to take everything that my people have but only a few of your kind are worthy of it and others will kill to get it. I must wait to be your wife my husband but I will be back forever."

Very shocked I wanted more than anything to expose these powers and punish them but how. Keeping the medallion hidden safely buried in a secret spot known only to me I carried on with my life as before doing nothing any different to any other person like myself and sure enough after about a year I became of no interest to anybody.

Chapter 2

It was now the year of 1983 and I had ceased seeing any blacked out windscreens on dark saloon cars in sight of me wherever I was and a new member of staff who had mysteriously joined the store where I worked right after meeting Karolla had left again meant that I was no longer of interest to anyone.
All the same I still held on to the hope that one day I would be hearing from either Orsat or better still from Karolla herself and as luck would have it pretty soon I did.

It was on a Wednesday afternoon toward the end of March that Whilst serving a young lady with a pushchair that I heard a voice in my head saying "I am so sorry that you have had to wait for so long without any contact from me my husband.

Father and I are here to show you how you can keep in contact with us without others knowing and how I can be at your side always." Glancing up I saw her standing back about four feet from me hands held onto a wheelchair with a much older looking Orsat sat it.

With my regular straight face look becoming one of great happiness as if I had suddenly won a lottery jackpot "No one is going to care about a woman and an old man my new son to be. Let us wait in your home for you.

We have so much to tell you there including about your mother." passing them the key to my home as it was they left heading out of the store and I elated continued working while counting down the minutes before finishing work and almost running to get home again.

Getting there I was ever so thankful that I was welcomed by them wearing normal everyday clothing but I did notice the fact that both of them wore gloves like every time that I had ever seen them before so I sensitively enquired as to why this was so to which looking first at her father and then back at me Karolla very and a bit reluctantly slowly pulled first her left then right glove off to reveal her only three fingered hands saying this is our natural look.

I could sense the fear in her talk on sharing this with me but her apprehension soon turned to relief when I said "Well I hope that this will not prevent you from kissing your husband my wife" With this and with no hesitation she flung her arms around me and kissed me with such complete love that I truly felt as if electricity was slowing through me.

That done Orsat said "If you sit down son I will tell you about your mothers" "Mothers how many do you think I have?" I asked Signalling with his eyes to Karolla who took hold of my hand he said "My wife bless her was killed during a fight with our old enemies many of your years ago against the ancient race who destroyed your neighbours on the planet you call Mars but your birth mother was impregnated by us with some DNA mixed with your own race in the hope that your children would discover your own origin and be able to stop what happened about 300 million of your years ago to you."

I was so shocked by this news that I wanted to cry out in anger but I knew that I had to keep calm asking "Does anybody else know all this and if so what is being done about it?" "Yes those in power and certain academics who are putting themselves ahead of the uninformed rather than admit their own past mistakes and failings." "Oh I guess keeping the status quo is closing the minds of many and of course greed for wealth power and control still after thousands of years of history. I guess nothing chances with human kind." I replied.

Karolla looking sadly down seemed to say the right thing when she asked if my species would ever put our future children and the Earth first adding maybe we should leave this plant for a new one. There are so many that you would love. Then Orsat ended with," Your kind do have a good chance for so much more as long as all your different religions believes and faiths accept that you are all humans despite your differences which should be your strengths."

We our brief listing of our faults we had to say bye to Orsat because he had to return to their spacecraft which was on the dark side of the moon away from prying eyes disappearing with a bright flash of light.

With it getting dark Karolla taking a hold of my right hand and lovingly led me to my bed seductively saying "I want us to send this night together my husband. "To which I obviously was in full agreement with her.

That night I made the most beautiful love with a woman from a different world from my own and truly felt more alive than ever knew that I could ever be. As we lay in each other's arms I breathed in a scent that came from out of her skin that increased my own feelings, it was like magic.

During this night I was able to ask the countless questions that were in my head such ask why she looked exactly like other human women except for her having only three fingers. "On our home planet that is how our race have grown over all time does it frighten you?" "I should be after growing up all of my life with almost nothing but the movies portraying space visiting life forms as such bad things but I try to judge them by who they are and not what they are.

That is why I love you so much." What is your planet called and is it anything like the Earth?" "I came from a planet called Kanil many light years away from here and it is very much like yours but the life forms are different looking but much the same as to how they live.

We have ice caps, deserts and jungles like you our seas have wonderful live in without the pollution that you have here. Our planets leaders treat abuse of our lands as a deadly crime. That is why us and other life forms are coming here to help you to save your world from your wars and self-interests of a few. But aware that there are other bad races that want your world for themselves. That is a reason not to pollute your air because it's better for them to take over."

One more question that troubled me where was the occupants of the dark car who had tried to abduct her when we first met and more importantly why. "My father said he believes they are part of a secret group that are keeping knowledge of any non-human life hidden for their own unknown purposes and will kill anyone for it. She said telling me through her talk that she is quite scared of them and what they would do to her if caught by them.

Trying to ease her worry I put my hands on her hips pulling her to me saying, "Well my love you have been caught by me and I want to make love with you right now." "Yes my husband anything you say it is my pleasure to do what you want." she replied with a very eager and sensual tone in her voice that had me kissing the whole length of her body drowning myself in the heavenly scent that came from her skin when aroused sexually. About a few hours later cleaned up and dressed again including Karolla's gloves we decided to go for a walk around the village that I had grown up in to meet a few old friends.

It was whilst at one friends home that he came out with, "Seeing you two has made me remember the dodgy looking men who were around here a couple of weeks back. They knew all about you Mike as if they were police but to be honest they were definitely not dressed, all in black suits and wearing black sunglasses.

And another thing they were very interested in any females who you know. To me it seemed like you are being investigated by very suspicious types, are you involved in anything bad? "All I could say was, "No not that I know of unless my bosses are now selling illegal things but as my friend please say nothing about Karolla and our relationship." "I won't say a thing because even I can see the fear in your eyes at this. If you need help you know where I am mate."

Leaving there we were left in no doubt that we were both in danger from the MIB's and had a very good idea as to why. Getting back home again we had to sit down and talk seriously about what we should do now. Karolla determined that we would never be parted by any secret groups from anywhere brought up an idea with my help but we would need very trusted help to do so a big part of me did not want to for obvious reasons but. She said, "What if we show your friend exactly what I am could you trust him if we need his help? "A big part of me wanted not to for the obvious reasons but if ever we were to be free to live like normal people we must at least try, so getting onto my mobile I called my friend Steve and within a few minutes he arrived at my door.

Coming in my friend Steve saying, "I knew there is something that you can't tell me mate but I won't tell a soul whatever it is so come on speak out." as he took a place at my kitchen table opposite Karolla.

I started by telling him everything from the start and understandably expected doubt when I reached the part about her. Looking first at him and then at her I gave her a nod and handed over to her. "He is telling the truth and I am the proof if you need to see." As she looked back she pulled off both of her gloves letting him see for himself the alien life who I loved making him jump to his feet in total shock.

Once calmed down Steve understandably realizing

he was actually in the presents of an alien life form he I think was quite perplexed over the whole thing until she reassured him that she had and would never think of eating your head bringing a smile to his face. After she placed her hand on his, with that now open to him he was able to focus his mind on our problem after a couple of hours we decided to carry on as if we knew nothing. As an almost after thought Karolla would pretend that her hands were as a result of a birth defect.

We did agree on a way of honouring us, believe in love being be so much better than those human and aliens whose bias and stupid self wants for whatever reasons Believe it or not it was Karolla herself who clearly and rightfully put things into prospective when she said, "I do not understand how nations will find ways to kill each other instead of joining together to stop it and help or save those who need it most, because on my world there is no greater calling then to care about others." "Is that why you are with Mike to help him." asked Steve to which she replied with, "No its because he risked his own life to save from the MIB's not knowing first.

When my father found out and wanted to know what I wanted to do about it my heart had already decided that my life is now his." "Phewww do you have any sisters I can save to get a woman as beautifully perfect as you are?" he said in jest but was very happy for us and proud to have been the only person other than I to actually meet and know her. With that I heard a noise that I will always treasure, that of Karolla laughing something that I had not heard before being our serious circumstances.

For the next eight months it felt as though we had

escaped any more unwanted interest by any secret group, that is until the day that Steve walked up me whilst I was working and whispered. "I saw a dark car parked outside your place earlier mate. Where is Karolla is she okay." "Shit I was hoping that they had given up on us, but at least she is okay for now. Her father took her up into his craft so she could fill him in on what we are doing."

With that I raised my voice to the same level as everyone else in the store asking him whether he had any plans to attend a local function in a few weeks going on to say, I'm taking the disabled woman I know because she has had little chance in the past because of her condition." With that an elderly lady who was being served next to me came out with, "What a lovely young man you are thinking of a disabled person. God bless you both.

"Actually I want to marry her she means everything to me. She is so much more and better than society give her credit for." With that praise from a stranger did give me a boost of a kind. The elderly lady then asked if I minded sharing the nature of my disabled ladies condition to which I said, "It should not even be thought of she was born with a deformity in both hands that has given her only three fingers on each. But she has been treated so cruelty all of her life because of it." "I'm so sorry for her You must have been brought together by higher powers I'm proud of your young man."

With that my colleague who was serving her completed her order and handed it over with a thank you." That was bloody quick thinking mate" Said Steve as he turned to leave the store I was working in.

It was only about an hour after that that my store manager a pleasant man who was well liked and respected among all those who knew him called my name out over the stores announcement system asking me to report to his office. This I had no worries about as I was often asked to do overtime or switch a day off with another member of staff but this time I was to be met by something that nobody expects.

"Please come in Michael and take a seat so we can talk privately." A little worried about why I was being summoned I did as ask curious as to why I was wanted."

You are not in any trouble with me Michael your record with us has been second to none but I believe that you are being targeted by others I have no idea who they are I cannot help but feel concerned about their motive. I have only seen two men dressed in black like funeral directors but very sinister looking. Is there anything that you can tell me in case things start becoming bad for you"

Wanting to open up and tell what I knew I was very worried about the possible consequences on Karolla, Steve or myself I played dumb again and thanking him for his obvious concern departed from his office returning to the shop floor. The remainder of that day passed by with no problem until I left work in lighter sky's being early summer with the intention of stopping at a care home for the elderly on my way home.

Maybe I should have said more because whilst talking with my manager I saw on a badge that he wore on his jacket a hooked cross emblem the same as my Karolla. Could there be a connection in this or was it just a coincidence who knew but I made a mental note of it.

Admittedly this is not what I regularly do but after buying some fresh fruit and flowers for the residence I arrived at the care home and was immediately welcomed inside by the head carer who led me along a pleasant hall way to a large communal lounge.

Passing the flowers, I brought to an assistant to place in water for show I was surprised to hear the elderly lady who had only hours previously complimented me on my love of disabled woman. She straight away started introducing the other residences telling them what a special young man and how considerate I was saying, "Take a seat right here beside me young man and tell my friends about your young lady and when you will bring her to meet us."

Already feeling uncertain of why I was actually there I took a place in a comfy armchair not truly knowing what to say or do so when outside of the open door in the hallway a sudden flash of bright light told me that I would soon know.

"So when is your big day going to be young man and can I come? Asked Mavis as I got to know her name as. "We will like that very much" came the beautiful voice of Karolla as she walked into the room bringing such happy smiles from all there.

Once the initial excitement had calmed down one of the cares brought another chair for Karolla to sit asking how she had been able to enter the building but she was intently looking around the room before looking straight into the eyes of a man saying, "I have a message for you

Archie from your wife. She said do not suffer any longer I am here waiting for you in a wonderful place."

Archie a war veteran had been kept alive by machines in silence before looked up at her saying thank you before closing his eyes in a peaceful sleep. No one can ever say what happened that night but sometime before morning he passed away. She never did answer how she had entered the building but on that one night she had not only known a man was about to die but she gave him solace before going and that was more than he would have had otherwise. After promising Mavis and the staff that we would come again soon we departed contented that we had been of help when needed.

It was when turning a bend in the road close to home that my mobile announce a new text message for me so under the light of a street lamp in the darkening night I read it said watch out mate they're back again parked in a house parking space ready to drive out of. After letting Karolla know what his text said we paused where we were for a minute or two to consider our next move. Suddenly as if hit by a brain storm she came out with, "I know what we can do. But we'll need to talk with Steve first."

Knowing that my phone was being monitored I had purchased a new disposable one that was not registered with anybody for this reason, so I called him an asked if he could conveniently break down right across the parking exit where they were so that they could not follow us come morning but it would not stop them from knowing we were going home now. That sorted the two of us casually returned home again as like millions of other young couples do every day.

Just we reached my front door and before even touching it I looked very carefully at because remembering the older spy and mystery movies that I loved watching as a child I had placed a little hair straight the opening edge of the door letting me know if it had been opened before getting home and it had. I do know that movies are pure fiction and often appear to show things as real even when not but can still give little tips for use in reality.

Before inserting my door key, I whispered," Don't even talk about anything that may be used by others because they have probably placed listening things inside to catch you out." "What can we talk about husband?" she asked before suggesting we talk about our visit to the care home.

"I admit on my planet we have no knowledge of your weddings because when two people are in love they just do it for all of their lives and never change their mates. I want to marry you here as well as we did the first time we mated for ever as one. I will be very happy if Mavis can be there to see our happiness."

Holding a hand held scanner in her right hand she showed me some flashing red lights crossing over from left to right indicating the presence of unwanted monitoring by we knew who by.

Quietly we entered my home before switching on the radio and making a fresh pot of tea whilst discussing our plan to visit the care home again the next day after my finishing work, while at the same Karolla talked to me in my head about our plans of avoiding the secret watchers of us outside.

Plus, with us being aware of the attempt to monitor our every action she signalled to me that we should mate for a good few hours and let our watchers know what true love is which had me suddenly start to giggle out loud leaving them scratching their heads as to why.

The following morning just as planned our friend Steve very conveniently pulled his car right across the parking bay in front of the car with the men who were spying on us and set about trying to fix a fault that was not there giving us the time needed to leave unobserved by them.

Walking out of our village on our way to my work I was struck by just how beautiful it was and how the sheep in a field beside the road that we were passing all seemed to rush to the side as if wanting to join us, or should I say Karolla.

She in turn appeared to be communicating with them almost as if she herself could talk to them and understand their bleating. Everything felt so perfect and peaceful with her that I completely forgot that she was in danger from our unknown persons spying on us who must have known who we were and considered us a national threat or something worse.

I remember thinking how stupid they would feel knowing that they are the greatest danger to all on our planet through their own secretive way of acting because we are in no way any kind of danger and love our planet and all on it even them. Just as we were about to round the last bend in the road before entering the town we kissed goodbye before she vanished in a bright flash leaving me to go to work as normal.

Walking into the store I could see the glass window of the manager's office overlooking the shop floor with the silhouetted shapes of two figures talking to the manager himself and turning to look straight in my direction signalling caution.

As I was changing into my work cloths in the staff room I heard the door behind me open and close again as someone entered and blocking any exit for me.

I saw it was the manager himself wanting I believe to talk privately with me. "I have just had a visit from two men wearing black and I think that you know more than I about them than you want to or can share."

Turning his lapel with the hooked cross badge on straight again he said, "My associates and I have been protecting our future under God since his son died for our sins and we are preparing for his child to return. I know that you know who I'm referring to and I believe you are already in contact. We are ready to help when needed. Here take this it is my private number you can use" Having said that he calmly turned and exited the room leaving me dumbfounded by his words.

Chapter 3

Leaving my work on this day was no different to any other except for the fact that I was met both my love ready to visit the care home and the sight of the two MIB's standing across the road watching us so fed up with them I walked straight over to them and said, "Instead of following me like a couple of secret agents or spy's, you may as well join us and help to carry the gifts for the old folk that we are visiting."

To see their faces surprised at being identified while uncertain as to what to do by us was a sight that I will never forget Directing my words at Karolla I said, "These two gentlemen are going to help carry the bags of shopping we have for the home my love."

And very reluctantly one of them crossed over the road and took hold of three shopping bags that we were carrying. After giving us their undercover names Tim and Clive we all made our way to the care home where we were met by the head carer a plump middle aged woman called Susan and a junior helper to welcome our presents from all there.

The man calling himself Clive presented himself as genuinely happy seeing both of us freely giving our time to bring happiness to the elderly in their final years with us.

Handing Mavis several weekly magazines brought such a happy smile on her face she gave Karolla a kiss on her cheek that I'm sure I saw a tear appear in her eye. Tim who had been standing so sternly just inside the door to the lounge area clearly feeling uneasy at being there suddenly reached up his hand over his heart as he suffered an attack collapsing onto the floor panicking the staff and the residence alike at seeing this but all was not lost yet.

With a breathing mask over his mouth to aid until paramedics arrived to help him Karolla looking at me said in my head," I can save his life husband if you want me to."

Without hesitation I nodded my support to do it and she calmly squat beside him laid there gasping for air and placed the palm of her right hand directly over his heart as a bright yellow glow appeared to move from her onto him as his breathing returned back off from barely any to normal and his eyes opened again.

Helping him to his feet and moving an armchair over for him to sit on Clive said, "Thank you, you have just saved my friends life at the expense of revealing what you really are why?" It was Mavis who made everything so clear by saying, I truly believe that God has sent us an angel to look after us." With that the head carer cancelled the call for help and asked her junior to bring us all a fresh pot of tea.

With Tim an average height stocky built man knowing

that the so called threat and danger to this planet had just openly saved his life completely changed his opinion and now knew that he was living a total lie by his bosses his dementia completely changed toward us but mostly toward Karolla.

She had proven herself as more friend than foe and it was his own superiors who were unknowingly becoming the very threat that they were supposed to be defending our planet from.

After having a talk with Mavis about what she had just seen right in front of herself she promised to never talk about it to anybody but she insisted on being there to see us marry which we were proud to do.

As for the others I had a quiet word with Susan she agreed to talk to her boss find out if it was possible to get married there so that the patients could share in our special day which she thought would be a great thing to do for them.

Clive who had stepped outside during the earlier incidence had been giving a report to their bosses approached Tim talking quietly in his ear not knowing that Karolla could read his mind thus letting her know what they were being ordered to do regarding us and it obviously angered Tim who refused to follow orders.

On exiting the home, we left our watchers returning home as they walked back to where they had left their car and drove off away from us but Tim on leaving whispered to me, "Get away my friends because our bosses have ordered us to kill you both because you know too much of what they are doing behind the peoples backs.

They have made deals with other races to turn humans into dependant workers and soldiers to use for their own wars against other planets and some of your own leaders are getting to rich and powerful again like Hitler tried to do.

They are heartless, often breaking your own laws and even starting wars to sell weapons for mass killing for profit. If the world carry on letting them get away with it this planet will end up as dead as Mars is now." Going on he said "Your Karolla and you are now in great danger and I will be dead in hours for telling you this but I would have died before if not for her efforts saving me."

Wishing each other good luck he with his partner departed heading out of the town and we hoped to safety while we intended to return home, but were met with fire engines dosing down a fire after a convenient gas explosion in our home which never did have any gas to it.

This was as good a warning that we were in serious danger from a secret sect within those at the very top. So with just the cloths on our backs we set about avoiding and if possible identifying those involved against us. Even though I was scared to death at the thought of Karolla being harmed in any way I forgot for a while that my boss and his associates might be able to assist us more than I have ever contemplated or indeed wanted.

Sitting huddled up on a park bench keeping warm I first asked her if I should call my boss and let him know everything that had happened since leaving my work to which she reluctantly agreed. I rummaged through my jacket pocket until I found the folded up piece of paper with his number on and dialled it, "I think it's time that we meet and tell you what is going on and show you why my friend.

You can meet us on the park bench where I live but hurry we are in bad danger here." "On my way now Michael but if you can stay out of sight until I get there in about ten minutes."

So whilst I shimmied my way up a nearby tree to watch the road close by Karolla locked herself into the public toilet there somewhat scared and unable to even contact her father for any help knowing that if he tried to come here he would almost certainly be captured or killed. The loud screech of a car stopping and the sound of a door being opened after just nine minutes let us know that help had arrived so as quick as we could the two of us climbed into the back and the car sped off.

"Don't say anything yet until I get you somewhere safe from them." were the only words that either of us heard as we were driven through the narrowing countryside roads until now on a not much more than a farmer's track to a massive iron gate with security cameras strategically placed with 360-degree coverage when with a flash of his headlights the gate opened and we were driven in. Finding ourselves in a man-made cavern large enough to park a juggernaut we got out of the car still not exactly where we were but did feel safer after what we had seen and been told by Tim.

My boss walking around the front of his car said, "I

am so glad it was not you in your place" pausing to take a breath of air continued with, "I heard the news reports that the remains of two bodies had been found and think it was you two." Shocked by this news I asked, "Does this mean we are officially dead? What do we do now? And where can we go?" "For now you can both stay here. Oh my name is Josh Sinclair." he said pushing a hidden leaver on the wall opening a doorway into a long passageway back into the rock leading to a separate room with plastered walls and carpet with antique furniture. We took seats around an old circular oak table looking at our new friend as he sat opposite us reading a message on his phone.

"Why are they so against you both?" He enquired obviously not knowing who he was in the presence of but thinking that one or other of us was important for some reason.

Looking over at Karolla asking her in my head if she wanted to share all with him to which she in the same way replied that we had no choice, so pulling her gloves off said, "Now you know why they want me but I am not going to be experimented on by them not ever!" "Wow I had a feeling that you were in possession of secret papers or something like that. I would never have even thought that you had an alien with you.

How did you catch her pausing before continuing with sorry you obviously are not forcing her in any way to do anything and that explains why those MIB guys are so interested in you Michael? How did you make contact?" "All I did was fight off two guys who were trying to force her into a car against her will, had no idea who or what she is." "He risked his life to save me and I could not help but love him for it." came her response confirming her free choice to be here with me.

After sharing all things became much clearer for my boss us to relax more but we were still in another secret place be it to protect us. Is that how our lives will have to be just because a very good person is different from the normal folk.

By this time, it was after three in the morning and all of us needed to get some sleep so my boss pointed out a side room which was set out like a bedroom with a double bed that had once stood in the French royal palace. that we could use before entering another room for himself.

With so much having happened that day we both quickly fell asleep holding tightly onto each other totally forgetting about everything outside even Steve and Mavis at the care home and everybody that we knew. There must have been a lot of tears flowing among them.

"Well Michael the store is remaining closed to show respect at your deaths yesterday and there is a growing display of flowers where you apparently were killed and I have arranged for an autopsy to show the bodies found were you, because we think they were really the MIB's. The claimed gas explosion that killed you has really put the cat amongst the pigeons out there because everybody knows that you had no gas within streets of your place and there was no damage to your neighbours' houses." Public demands are being made for the truth about it."

Were the headlines in the press and on the TV and radio true?. The house of commons is trying to have it all explained way as trapped natural gas but some do not believe it. Is there anything that I can do for you now?" "I wish Steve and Mavis could be told that we are both alive but I guess its best that nobody knows anything for now for their sakes it is so sad." I said trying to think of our needs for now.

After writing a list of our needs including clothing, toilettes and personnel things my boss started making calls and making arrangements to get it all for us.

As for the last and most important thing for Karolla to let her father know that we were both alive and well we soon had the means to do just that thanks to our new friend Josh, I will never understand his means but leading us back to the first main room by pressing a remote control and the central table and chairs started dropping down further into the floor revealing a second floor with a central control centre with screens up on the walls showing television from everywhere worldwide.

"Is your father able to pick up radio signals" asked Josh to Karolla. "He should be able to pick one up but he won't answer in case it gives away his location." Directing our eyes to the screens on the wall he pointed out a tall tree on the top of a rock outcrop where we were saying that it was also a radio mast able to send signals into space. Using a sort of binary code, he sent this message 2okruok soon receiving a reply icuok, that was enough to let her know that her father was aware that she was okay.

I was so astonished by this especially as he was by all sakes just a shop manager on the normal wage how has he been able to do all this without it being known by anyone.

"I'm just wondering your name Sinclair is it any connection to the Henry Sinclair who was helping the ancient Templars escaping from the then pope?" "Possibly why do you want to know that? It was so long ago and the people will not cope with the truth that the Catholic church despite their many good things do have so much to answer for in keeping their control over lives worldwide by removing important parts of the bible like the book of Enoch, the Spanish inquisition, and helping Hitler and his top SS escape justice at the end of world war two to Argentina. Luckily the FBI are investigating that now.

Because I had in the past heard about this nook of Enoch I had downloaded it on my computer and was reading it and it has completely affected my own beliefs but to be honest I always try to follow the ten comments in my everyday life by doing what little I can to help the more needy than myself." On that Josh seemed to be taking it all in. "Now knowing that all that I believe in is my love for a non-earth born woman who not only healed my wounds after saving her but saving the MIB called Tim and willingness to live here on a different world for me."

Having done what, we had to we returned back up to the main room to discuss what we were going to do now. After an hour or two we only managed to think of a couple of ideas mainly the opinion of Karolla and maybe I as well leaving this planet for good which I admit selfishly was reluctant to do so we agreed to sleep on it a while and think about it.

After Josh had earlier shown us a fitted out kitchen area we took ourselves there to have something to eat talking about our situation as we did while Josh went out to get what we needed and get an update on the day before.

I cannot say where or why I came up with it but as we were kissing and watching the cooker grilling some toast I came out with" Baring in mind that we are now dead what do you think would happen if we suddenly appeared alive on television and revealed what is going on by the secret organisations who are trying to kill us for unknown reasons my love." "We can talk with Josh when he gets back but turn the grill off before it burns or let it burn and kiss me some more my husband." with that I finished off doing the toast so we could at least eat before going to bed.

On his return Josh was able to hand us what we needed before settling us down to hear his news about us and our apparent deaths. "Well I guess you want to know what is happening out there. I have figured out that you Karolla must have had a great effect on the folks in the care home by your presents because the impact of losing you has upset all of them including the staff.

The resident Mavis swears that you are an angel sent to help them when their time comes and the head carer is telling everyone how you saved a man's life in front of all of them just by placing your hand on his heart.

And as for you Michael they talk about how you gave your time to visit and bring them gifts." The town's main church is going to hold a special service at your funerals so it's probably wise not to go." "Thank you Josh for doing this for us." I replied with still unsure as to what we can do about our situation. "Oh those MIB guys I think must have been the ones killed in your place because their car has been found nearby. I'm wondering if they killed themselves to protect you both because they knew that you are good people and it's their leaders who are being very bad for unknown reasons."

"I wish that I had known because my father could and would saved them and relocated them elsewhere to start a new life. That's it my love we can move to a different land, or even another planet if you want." she said holding tightly to my hands.

Pulling her closer to me I said, "I'll be honest love I love this planet and its life but if the only that we can be together means leaving here I will but at the same time I would feel a traitor to my own kind." "I understand my love but your kind will make all life extinct within three generations if you carry on as you are anyway.

We can begin a new Earth somewhere out there just think we could be a new Adam and Eve and make lots of babies together." kissing me ever so lovingly I do admit the idea of that was very tempting but I could not just leave my home without at least trying to help to save us from ourselves but how can an officially dead person do anything?

Chapter 4

With the help of Josh and his camcorder we all got to witness our own funerals beside each other in a local churches graveyard and the large crowd of people wanting to pay their respects.

I truly felt humble seeing Mavis placing a pure white rose on each of our coffins and bowing her head in prayer in her belief that we were indeed dead. Scrutinizing the watchers there he pointed out two MIB figures stood back and watching everyone there who were definitely not Tim and Clive telling us that they knew it us not us being buried there.

This was proof enough that we were still in great danger for nothing more than my being in love with an alien born visitor to our planet as others people around the world also are but in my case I know that I am.

"I think that we may be able to let Mavis know we are alive." said Karolla peaking our attention straight away knowing that she had ability's unknown to others.

"Remember how the first time we talked to each other was through thought direct into your mind. If I can get a direct line of sight with her I could tell her not to be too sad because we are still here and alive but she must never say because we are in danger." "Why would you risk doing that." asked Josh somewhat confused as to why she would risk so much for an elderly human woman. "Because I could feel the pain in her loss and she does not deserve it." so we agreed to.

A week later Josh with Karolla disguised to hide her appearance sitting in the back of his car pulled in beside a public garden with an outside tea area and waited to see her having a regular drink and cake in the open air. Being pushed in a wheelchair by a career and looking as if her mind had almost given up on life, she was stopped luckily for us facing the parking area where they were waiting so Karolla sending her our message. "Mavis do not do anything but we need to tell you that Michael and Karolla are alive and miss you ever so much.

I loved the white roses that you put on our graves but we cannot see you yet. Cheer up honey we will all be together when it is safe for us. I am in the car in front of you." With that she slowly raised her face up and smiled. With that they pulled away returning to our hideaway happy that Mavis was returning to her normal bright and bubbly self.

The very next day we received confirmation that if it was the MIB's that blew up my home to kill us to hide the truth they would not have needed to exhume Karolla's coffin that same night and then returned for mine the same night. That told us that there must be another party after her but for what reason and why?

The only thing that we could of thought of was perhaps they found out that our coffins actually had the bodies of Tim and Clive in meaning that we were still alive and knew what they were doing. Or we could not ignore the possibility that there was an unknown party who are themselves after her.

We had no idea what to do at this point but as became apparent to us keeping informed of unexplained news when eye witnesses reported seeing a craft crashing on an unpopulated area about fifty miles away from us.

Apart from a sudden increase of military activity and a news blackout the public were told that a piece of space debris had fallen to Earth but we knew otherwise. Luckily for us the local television briefly showed the film footage taken by a police officer on patrol in the same area before it conveniently vanished as did the officer in question. Fortunately for us an associate of Josh had recorded the film footage allowing us to see it enabling Karolla to it which frightened her greatly.

"It's the planet who want to marry me off to force my world to let them have your world for its abundance of ore that they need for their weapons and space craft. Your leaders do not know what they are after." The whole Galaxy is in more danger than you know and yours and my own home will end up like Mars is now. You are not alone in this we must tell the world that our friends up there must unite to save us all."

"Why do they want to marry you off to get here because you are now my wife and not theirs." Well basically her forefathers about five thousand years ago discovered Earth and its ancient life and saw the potential in you so stayed living with and as humans while improving your DNA.

Somewhere along the way some of my race loved, married and mated with your kind and our DNA's began joining up until now, but we decided to mostly leave you to grow up by your own efforts, the few who did stay have as good as become a part of you and are the same in every way even to the extent of forgetting who they as it should be. The Ruffians think that if they marry me off to one of their own they will own the Earth and all on it, but we can never let them."

Being told this sent a chill right up through me leaving me wondering what she meant by ending up like Mars is now. "Mars was just like here with animals, plants, water and a breathable atmosphere until 300 million of your years ago they used atom explosions in the air killing everything there to take possession but they could not get it because the air was poison to them so they went elsewhere but have found about your planet by your nuclear explosions this last century and long in your own past and also know about my kind and me."

"Why about you what makes you important to them?" I asked. "Because on my world I am a sort of princess but not like here."

"My God what chance have we got against odds like that, is there any chance for us." "To be honest my father says there is not unless you all stop making the air pollution and warring against each other over religion or belief.

Your leaders know this but are afraid or have been stopped from doing the right things to save yourselves. Your youth today are becoming aware of all this but unable to do more than protest which is ignored by politics that value wealth over life. If your NASA and other people were to tell all that they finding out maybe nations would work together to help solve your problems for all on the Earth and truly honour your Gods."

That night I actually cried myself to sleep thinking about everything that Karolla had told us and I know that Josh was as upset as I realizing that humans are in an uncaring way killing ourselves and the whole planet because of petty self-interests and greed, want of power and in many cases control. So what we have different skin colours. Beliefs, sexual preferences and other differences but we all breath the same air and bleed the same colour blood. meaning that we are all human beings with a duty under our Gods to help each other.

Come morning as we all ate breakfast of toast, fresh fruit and a cup of tea we made plans for the day including a bit of shopping for the necessaries like food in a town further away from our home town and for Josh contacting his trusted associates across the pond in America who are already aware of the use of lying to keep secrets from everyone including their own people as all powers do.

As for Karolla and I she by her own admission was scared to death at the thought of being seen by the wrong persons and held onto my hand so tight that I actually started losing the feeling in it. This I partially eased by keeping her mind on her hopes and dreams of our married life and any children that we may be blessed with as well as her natural connection with wild life in general. I ended up promising to let her choose a pet when everything was all over and done with.

"Just a thought you guys what if we could have a talk with the MIB folk and work together instead of them trying to kill you that might be beneficial to all concerned after there will never be a threat to anyone on Earth from you." said Josh while talking to whoever on his phone meaning us.

"We can warn them about the Zoffians and their plans against us." Thinking about it we were sceptical of the whole idea to start with because we could not guarantee that they would not lie and double cross us for their own purposes. All the same if we did not at least try we would as good as be signing our planets death warrant so set about planning to make contact with them. The first thing we decided to do was to give them a reason to be at a certain place at the right time and isolate one only to start with.

Three days later as Mavis was having her regular afternoon drink at the outdoor garden cafe she was handed a card by a waitress telling her to expect a visitor that evening signed her angel which she knew instantly who angel was. As hoped the carer must have seen or read the card and informed her superior because the car park of the care home was filled newspaper and, TV reporters, the police and obviously a dark green saloon car with darkened windows plus a small crowd of curious general public.

At six pm a car driven by my best friend Steve pulled up and I got out and at the same time there was who at first appeared to be a nurse getting out as well walking into the home as if we were only staff and a visitor.

A loud cheer and clapping emitting from inside soon had those outside trying to barge in but were prevented from getting in by the police outside until one reporter who had reported on our claimed deaths and funerals recognised who we actually were telling all which sprung up calls for answers.

So surrounded by staff and residences alike we stepped out in full view of the press and others holding hands to speak out, "Where have you been, why have you not spoken yet, who was it that died in your home, why is there no record that your wife even exists and what are you hiding from us and who removed the coffins from your graves."

"Okay okay I know that everybody wants to know the truth but for now it is best that I restrict myself to answering as much as I can without endangering the lives of good people world over caught up in secret matters. About a year ago I unknowingly saved the life of a young woman who was being attacked by two men.

As a result, she saved me after one or other attackers slashed across my back and stabbed me. Those two men were paid agents by an unknown International group hiding secrets from everyone around the world because they are afraid of the consequences of us knowing the truth.

As it turned out one of the men was saved after a bad

heart attack almost killed him by the very person he was paid to kill, my now my wife princess Karolla.

One of you asked about her because there is no record of her even existing that is because she is not Earth born. And that is why whoever they are wanted to kill her.". "Are you trying the play some sort of sick joke with your Alien ET stuff. To excuse away the desecration of your supposed grave and those buried in them.?" came a sceptical comment off one reporter. "And that is exactly what those in power are or will already be inventing as excused to cover up the truth from us all."

That sir is what they want you all to think but I am only talking to you now because the bodies exhumed from our claimed graves were in fact those two paid killers who would not kill their saver and so bravely blew themselves up in my home to save us killing themselves in doing so."

After several staff and residences of the home publicly confirmed what was said about the MIB's and how one had been saved by Karolla with it actually caught on security cameras inside the home with unofficial copies made after the original was taken by them were handed to the press. I finished off with this plea, "After telling a small amount of what I know and knowing that even our own Government will be after us for whatever reason they can think of now we will both be vanishing from view but still here doing what we can to help you all.

God bless you all thank you." turning quickly to run back into the care home before sneaking out of a rear fire escape to be driven off fast by Steve.

Chapter 5

With my giving the interview on camera and giving the press camera footage showing Karolla's willingness to reveal who and what she is to save a human males life, who had been ordered to kill her filled almost every newspaper and TV news channel all of the day repeating what I said about the government wanting to disclaim it all as a hoax. That proved true to form quickly done but not believed by many off the public. Even the current pope publicly stated that if alien life came here the church would welcome them into the church. That we hoped would open the door to our alien friends to visit us as friends, wanting to help to save us all but the very rich and powerful parties and leaders just carried on with their self-interests ahead of our planets increasing needs.

Even the worlds militaries to an extent are rightly putting their national security first but there is no planetary security with all nations equally involved as we as a planet need much more than making more destructive and deadly weapons to use on each other and sell for profit.

As for us we hope with all our hearts that those in power will pull their heads out their own arses and admit that we are all nothing as we are but can be so much more working together for our planet. All it should take is one big power to freely give needed help to another or even all in friendship.

Keeping ourselves out of any contact with the outside world in Josh's hidden underground cavern we were able to stay in touch with global news and search for me and my claimed alien that the press was ordered to call student hoaxer backed by corrupted experts and scientists. When a new TV serial called ancient aliens appeared in the UK from America we truly hoped that enough people would start demanding tax payer paid governments force the truth to be released to the public because after all they are paid by the people and as such can be sacked or even tried for withholding or miss using public funds. The best thing about this series is how it asks what ifs while leaving it to the watcher to take what they want from it.

It felt strange to me how even with live film proof of alien space craft from around the world our leaders still deny there are countless other planets that can and do visit ours for their own reasons, some bad but more good. I understand how most people are reluctant to accept this because they had not seen anything themselves just like myself before my actually seeing one myself. None the less if never seen animal species can live and thrive here does that mean does that mean they do not exist until we all see them.

That would be stupid so why are our leaders so intent on denials and cover ups even when they know the truth.

This way of thinking is likely to do greater harm to us all than any good.

For Karolla and I it was becoming very clear that what we know has given us a death sentence by those secret groups that are afraid to release their controls over the people that for centuries they have had.

Profit, power and control is more in significant to them than the lives of common people and that is a massive insult to the Gods that they swear to and worship.

As for us we became very aware of it when checking the local papers and read about the mysterious sudden death of our friend Steve falling off a cliff that he has never seen or had reason to visit before. This news I believe was a message to us that our very existence is a threat to their ideals.

"That is enough my love. It is time to leave my home planet and go to your planet or anywhere with you so we can live as a normal loving married couple for our future children." I stated in my upset over my friend's murder by my fellow human beings. "No! That is not who you are.

This is and will always be our home. We have to prove that we must push aside petty differences and make a better world that can a million years and not the dead world we are allowing to happen for selfish greed by some." she quite angrily proclaimed humbling me because after all she was right. I think it was more curiosity that made me ask but I said, "What makes you love this planet so much is it the wild life, fish filled seas, the birds in the sky or what?" "Apart from you my everything" with a loving look in her eyes, "It is the way that your ancestors built and left so many lessons for you to learn from to avoid making their own mistakes.

Your planet is a living history lesson. for you all to understand to become better. You are able to not only read about but actually see and touch and in a way I envy them. My world was almost destroyed billions of years ago but was saved by our planet friends. That might be why we have always been here for you."

A ringing on her phone instantly grabbed our attention as nobody even knew that she had one other than Josh and I and he was there with us. Taking a look at it she straight away admitted that she had given it to Mavis in case of an emergency

She had been sent a voice mail saying, "One of those men in blacks needs to see you anywhere any time be. She is here as a carer so they can talk with you and knows that you are good. and no threat to us" "How can we believe that after Steve's death are they trying to trick us into going out so they can kill us as well? I replied to her.

"But if it is true and he was killed by others?" she said in a positive hopeful way. So I suggested that if I alone went to the home and saw Mavis I could get a better idea of if it would be safe for her.

After a night of talking about any possible dangers we decided that with the help of Josh he would drop me off at the home and stay in the car outside ready to speed off if we had to. We talked a lot whilst travelling to the home about what to do if there was any trouble regarding protecting

Karolla in the event of it being a double cross just to get her. Stepping into the home I could not see or even sense anything out of place so I handed Mavis a bunch of flowers from us like any visitor would do.

After a normal little bit of chit chat about she beckoned over one of the female carers introducing me saying "This is the wonderful husband to be of my darling angel Karolla." "I know who Michael is. I am very happy to meet you. Can we have a little chat in private please."

Stepping out of the room and sitting on one of the chairs placed along the side of the public hallway the carer called herself agent Angelina a fit and well-shaped woman with a dark service cut hair began with, "I've seen your television return from the dead and heard what you said.

And I saw your wife's saving of one of my colleges thank you for saving Tim was a good friend of mine. Now we need your help because our American friends have tracked several unknown craft entering our space and entering the UK's air space. We know that they are a threat because NASA filmed them firing at a point on the dark side of the moon before a graft flew up and off." Hearing that my thoughts were instantly about Orsat and if he was okay.

"They might be the Zoffians, and they are definitely the threat you thought my wife is I must see her." standing up and rushing back out to Josh's car. We have to get back mate Karolla might need us and her father has been attacked from what I've just been told.

Getting back we were met by Karolla throwing her

arms around me clearly upset and frightened. "What has happened my love. Are you okay?" "I am now; I've been so scared that they might have killed you as well like Steve."

Kissing so lovingly she relaxed not knowing the facts which Angelina had shared with me which I knew would hit her hard with worry about her father. With my arm around her I directed her to the underground control centre and sat her down to give her the news.

As I relayed what I was told she calmly said, "That is exactly what my father would do to draw them away from here to give us more time to prepare for our fight back. We have many friends out there who are certainly helping him, but we must be aware that their agents are already here working their lies against you. Tim's order to kill you both was just like them using you against yourself so that after you have another world war they can take your planet over and some of political and religious powers are not knowingly helping them."

With that our attention was suddenly refocused up onto the ceiling of our hidden underground cavern by a flashing red light alerting us to a presence outside at the entrance iron gate. On checking the security camera covering it we saw a dark saloon MIB car drivers side door opens and of all people Angelina standing there waiting under an umbrella with quite persistent rain coming down for someone to appear. "What do I do." asked Josh clearly concerned that his secret cavern might have been revealed. "It's your choice my friend, let her in or hope she goes away not knowing where we are."

"I've got an idea. I have another way in from the clump

of trees to the left and can appear as an ordinary guy just out taking a casual walk just like anybody else does."

So while Karolla and I watched on the big camera screen we nervously watched as Josh wearing muddy clothing and carrying a bag with freshly picked apples clambered out of the trees and climbing through a small gap beside the gate acting surprised at seeing her by her car.

"Please don't say you're the farmer and I'm in trouble for scrimping your apples." asked Josh innocently. "You know that I'm not, I want to see your friends not where you are hiding them. I know they are nearby and I don't give a shit what or who you are I just need to see them. Michael knows who I am." "Okay stay there and I'll ask." Disappearing back into the trees behind him Leaving her standing there trying not to get to wet from the rain.

About ten minutes later a mechanical sounding clunking noise signalled the slow opening of the gate as if rust had seized it up its workings years before. Almost jumping out of her skin in surprise she had an Earth shaking shock when the solid rock before her started opening inward like a door and Josh and I were standing inside to welcome her. "Come with us and meet Karolla my wife."

I said looking at her opened mouth astonishment at what she was witnessing before her. "How how how have you done all this without anyone else knowing. Do your government and military know?"

"It was started by lord Sinclair in the thirteenth century for the tenplers before their crossing to America and has been improved over all these years for me to continue guarding our lord's treasures and secrets." added Josh. Removing her rain soaked long coat I could see her taking as much information in as she could be remembering everything for future use if wanted.

"You must be Angelina I am pleased to meet you" said a voice as Karolla stepped into the light of where we were from a side passage on the back wall. Holding her hand out to shake hands Angelina hesitated in responding at the sight of her three fingered hand but rose above her uncertain trained way to shake quickly finding a sense of friendship quite different to what she was taught to think.

"Come with us and warm up after being out there in this weather. You can have a hot drink as well and eat something if you want, we have it all here." "How long have you known about this place. And where are the men?" she asked just like an investigator would do.

"My husband and I only found out about here after his home was blown up and Josh hid us from you MIB's." Yes, I am sorry for that Tim confided in me about you saving him by risking your own life, that's why I am on your side here. My superiors are working on their own agendas and it is wrong." "I do not know what is happening, I just hope Josh and my father have a good idea what to do." said Karolla trying to give a little support and shared worry to our new friend. "Your father is alive and well now Karolla." announced Josh entering the room where we were looking very relieved at his news. "How do you know that?." she asked hugging me in celebration but for how long will it be before we get more trouble from them.

"I cannot say for sure but the craft chasing your father

was destroyed passing Jupiter by an ally from the Orion's belt star system they were waiting for them so your father can come back to you as long as our powers do not prevent it like usual for their own interests.

It is a shame that your planet security is ignored for national benefits, but at least one day you may learn." "What about the Zoffians now?" I asked hopeful of good news regarding them, but I was not and as I was to learn later even my life was in great danger from both the Zoffians and powers here on the Earth but why I had no idea.

Chapter 6

After our updating Angelina with what we knew she promised to keep secret any information about Josh and our involvement with him and his help f or us knowing that even her bosses wanted us dead so that they could cut us up for any biological gains that may be acquired from our bodies. As it was although Karolla and I were now able to communicate telepathically with each other I did not have the ability to read others thoughts but could in a way transmit face to face as when I was able to talk to Mavis.

It was a late morning that a signal was picked by Josh's radar equipment letting was know that we were about to receive a visitor who would be able to answer some of our questions our predicament relating to our being hunted by our own people. Sure enough it was while I was trying to get Karolla to tell me why she had suddenly acquired a taste and craving for porridge mixed with fresh strawberries and served with ice cream. I did have a suspicion but with her not being Earth born there may have been a different reason for this change in her habits.

With the expected bright flash of light, we were joined by another member of her race baring a message from her father in that he was up in space developing an early warning system in case the Zoffians tried taking her again along with several other planets but would have been more if our own military's did not treat friends as foes just because we are so far behind them and stupidly believe that we can do anything without outside help.

Our leaders need to publicly admit we are being visited from outer space and set landing areas for our friend's crafts to land openly and safely in full knowledge just like an airport does for our aircraft. We know that whichever nation is intelligent enough to do it first will show the rest of the world that now in the 21st century we are able to see the big picture and be mature enough not to kill each other for our differences. It's those differences that will one day save us all.

I will admit that our visitor looked strange with his long thin arms and legs due to the gravity where he came from, his big skull, almond shaped eyes, lack of ears and just a marrow slit for a mouth was obviously so proud bowing when Karolla spoke to him and signalling to us all to sit around the central Oak table.

Being used to her longer three fingers I had no difficulty in shaking hands with him knowing that he was here to give us wanted news. "I have been told to let you know why you also are being hunted down by your own powers." started our visitor aimed directly at me, "It is because with your father being unknown and your mother refusing to give his name and lie all the time plus your having the ability of some telepathic ability they think your DNA may have a part of that of Jesus.

I am sorry but if you do it will have become so little during the last two thousand years it will be worthless to anybody. The connection with her highness is more from her than you." "Your highness? Just how important are you my love."

I asked straight at Karolla who was busy eating porridge mixed with strawberry's and ice cream to which with a slight blush replied with, "I've passed my position on to my sister so our child can be born here with both of its parents." Well that answered my questions having me dropping on to my knees and declaring my total love for her and devotion to our coming baby.

And turning to our visitor said, "Do not let it be known yet until we know if our child will develop as hoped as a hybrid of our peoples but however it comes out it is our baby." Hearing her say that filled my eyes with great pride in her. I found it hard to belief that without knowing her before a woman from another planet had fallen in love with me of all men just for trying to stop two men from abducting her.

After I had come back to the ground from the clouds after my fantastic news I suggested giving a sample of my blood to our own MIB's on the condition that they leave us alone unless we wish otherwise which surprisingly was agreed but I still doubted it being kept to. The following day a Wednesday Josh drove us both to the care home so that we could tell Mavis our news.

With that she was so happy for us wanting to be its first

visitor and if it is a girl to name it after her, something that Karolla had been thinking herself due to her calling her an angel. On telling her the head carer plus without exception wish us nothing but good wishes and others to baby sit while we celebrate our new family. Even Jolene who was still undercover there was excited for both us and my other of blood with unusable DNA.

With all that now sorted out we were finally able to find a new home, this time with access to an area of clear land just in case Karolla's father wanted to land. Something hoped for knew could not be as yet. So you can imagine the pain I felt when after her telling me that whilst our child was growing inside of her it would be dangerous for her to be taken up into any spacecraft she just vanished without warning from outside of a property that we had just viewed.

Knowing just how two faced and some of our secret sects can be I was on the phone to Josh to check on if Jolene was still here. " Yes she is with me right now, why do you ask?" came his reply.

"Someone or thing has just taken Karolla, she just disappeared with no warning." Pausing a second or two before adding," However it was has just made the worse mistake ever cos I want to kill them." "Where are you, we are coming but try not to kill em all I want a go as well she is far too good to lose." About half an hour. later they arrived both red faced in anger and wanting to lash out at whoever was responsible.

Straight away Angelina put her arms around me for a comforting hug while Josh himself turned on radar tracking to identify the source and method of taking her but there was nothing to see. It was almost as if she had just been removed from existence.

"I've contacted our visitors craft and told him. Now I can't but wonder if he may in some way be involved because she was safe and protected here until he left. Either he was somehow tracked her or I hate to say it but it might have been him especially as he had just discovered that she is pregnant with your hybrid child. There must be secret groups on her planet bent on their own agendas. The Zoffians do not have the technology to do this that we know of."

"I was able to track you with our limited technology so why couldn't other alien races because they must be so much better than us, but who?" added Jolene. "That's what I am thinking myself." I answered trying not to break down in tears at my empty feeling without her. I was unable to think to clearly in my emotional state, but I was not alone in my loss as Josh had himself grown a love as a father figure to both of us which we valued.

"I know what we can do for now. If you go to work Joe and find out anything that might help especially from your bosses. I will be in contact with my friends all over and check out any chatter online." With that we all set out in different directions but with the same intent to find and bring back my wife and unborn child.

My first stop was the store where I worked before my apparent death being welcomed by staff members wanting to know how Karolla and I were and were mostly concerned for her when I shared my news with them.

As I walked along this first aisle and around the corner into the next one I caught a glimpse of a man dressed in black looking at a mobile phone and talking through a microphone which had me expecting more trouble. Just as I was about to grab him and start demanding my love be returned but that never happened because the black suit I saw was an undertaker on a break from his work.

Leaving the store again I just walked about aimlessly with nowhere to go or even caring where I was going inevitably ending up at the care home where Mavis and the staff could tell that something was wrong with me. After explaining the situation to them Mavis gave me a massive hug and asked to keep her up to date with things because she missed her angel.

"They are back, the Zoffians know that Karolla is with child and want to get one or both of them they have infiltrated high places with new technologies that appear to help but actually help the turning of your air deadly to you while turning the planet ideal for them. Billions of your people will die before those at the top accept he facts.

Too many worlds have made the same mistake including my own several billion of your years ago. That is why some of us are trying to help you. Oh your wife and daughter are okay and safe while we sort out the Zoffian problem my son." came a very clear voice in my head it was from her father letting me know that my love was safe and more importantly I had become a father.

In the late spring whilst he was talking with his MIB contact we became aware of a new deadly virus that was worrying more than one planet as in, is it natural or a type of biological weapon developed by who knew.

It was not until the following year 2019 that we got proof that some biological life does live and travels in space and that was very worrying, so when a new one was discovered in China the world slowly but cautiously began changing the ways that we all live our lives.

By the January on Earth the virus was named as Covic19 a corona virus that had crossed species to our own affecting the whole world and killing countless people. More than that Karolla's father was even more concerned about a planet known to him as Cruxen a small planet about twice the size of the Earth's moon and the first known victim of this new virus killing about 80% of over two billion inhabitants. The first thing that the Cruxen scientists discovered was that only their own species was affected from all life forms there.

As I passed this information on to Karolla I could clearly see the deep upset in her eyes with a sense of fear especially knowing that this virus was appearing here on our home planet as well "Well it is here now. I pray that our leaders realise that the self-interests of different countries come together for all being infected and dying to soon.

Viruses never stop at national borders and ignore human differences such as belief, location, age and even gender my love." Brushing the tears away from her eyes she asked, "With all that we have learnt during last few years I wander if the MIB's or Josh have any more news."

After calling Josh and letting him know our intention of going to his secret hidden base he assured me that he would be watching and waiting for us to arrive. Climbing into my car an old red Toyota I switched on the radio listening to the continuous claim and counter claim from all over the planet as each Country chose to blame another mainly China because the virus was first identified as appearing there, but not one single acknowledgement that it may be from outer space and able to cover the globe by infecting humans who travel all over thus spreading the rising death total.

Even with no way to stop or even slow its progress every nation was to begin with understandably more concern with carrying on trading and making profit at first until the death toll made us all re-evaluate our lives. In every Country for obvious reasons Governments began locking down everything as they battled the effects on everyone and finding ways of hopefully beating this planetary disease that was targeting only humans here and human like life on other worlds rising worry the it may be an attack, but for what reason.

If it is possible to note one benefit from the outbreak, it must be to massive reduction in all the pollution that as a species we have been creating in our air and in our seas without consideration beyond profit and self-interests that every one of us has been guilty of for many reasons in the past. I personally hope that when we get through this our leaders and business put the whole planet and its environment first.

For myself my main priority was my wife and child as well as my good friends and neighbours. With my update from my friend Josh, our contacts in the MIB's and the secret friends protecting world ancient treasures and

Karolla's alien race doing all that they can to help our race beat the virus travelling through space.

I needed inside to hold her close to me and our boy Leaving Josh's secret hidden base inside of a hill via a seldom used trackway sheltered by its high tree lined hedges I remembered how with his help both of us would have been killed in order to get and try to used her DNA by the military for their own purposes under the guise of national security.

Luckily all that worry was laid to rest when Karolla revealed her true identity by saving the life of a MIB agent ordered to kill her on camera for all to see, that is until those in power came up with excuses and lies to cover up the truth as they always do.

Just as I rounded the last gentle turn in the track toward the joining of the much quieter roadway ahead the head lights of another vehicle coming toward me lit up the trackway before me double flashing its lights and pulling to a stop before me. Once stopped we could see it was a MIB dark saloon car driven by our contact with them Angelina signalling to stop before getting out of her car and approaching me. Looking very concerned she said, "My friend, do not return to your home, you are both in danger Ataya is safe for now, he is being cared for by a Templar colleague ".

All that I could do was turn around and return to Josh's secret cave complex hidden behind and in the granite rock hill. "At least we can breed more to keep us busy." said Karolla snuggling close to me not showing the deep concern for not just our friends but for all.

After following me back through the massive iron gate, before pausing while the whole rock wall opened and closing again once we had driven in showing absolutely nothing this was to be the start of many months of lock down for the whole UK. and all other country's meaning streets everywhere were mostly bare of traffic allowing the air pollution drastically reduced on the good side but was largely unseen and to an extent ignored.

On entering the cave, we were to become aware of an unknown fact withheld from the popules in the fact that some UFO craft are invisible to the eye but can be filmed on Invar red cameras. This fact was revealed when a Chilean camera operator by accident did and released it to the world press but still more or less ignored by the people unable or unwilling to accept that the Earth is not the best planet in space even when undeniable proof is found.

What is even more revealing being the proven fact that at a place called Skin walker ranch in America when a team of five experts including Travis Taylor PHD a sceptic not only saw two UFO's with their own eyes, filmed it and scientifically recorded the whole thing. "I can understand why our religions, faiths and believes have for centuries have even started wars against others to hide or even deny the truth for their ends but they are betraying the Gods that they pray to, because God must know about or perhaps even be from elsewhere in space.

What do you think? I asked out loud not really knowing why I was even thinking what I was saying to no one in particular and not expecting a reply. "You are closer to the truth than you will ever know my husband." came Karolla's reply to me.

Getting back into the command centre we found a recorded message from Josh letting us know that he was under lock down because several staff members where he worked had tested positive for the corona virus but for now he was well but a little scared after so many were dying from it.

Ending his message, he confirmed that China was being blamed for the virus simply because the first cases were reported there but as we knew came from outer space giving rise to all sorts of lies and false claims for political self-interests by corrupt leaders, and finally for Karolla her father Orsat had said that other planets were looking to others for any natural immunity that may be able to protect all lives against this invisible enemy.

It is well known that every country rightly has its own national security but when will there be an open International planetary security organization that will prevent any one person, party or nation from risking the lives of innocents for their own political, financial or personal benefit, because unless there is the threat of another world war will only grow for us all. When that is done respecting each other's ideals and beliefs our societies deserve or maybe not be welcomed by the alien life's that have been secretly helping us evolve over the countless centuries to be better than we are.

It is well known that every country rightly has its own national security but when will there be an open International planetary security organization that will prevent any one person or party from risking the lives of innocents for their own political, financial or personal benefit, because unless there is the threat of another world war will only grow for us all. When that is done respecting each other's ideals and beliefs our societies deserve or maybe not be welcomed by the alien life's that have been secretly helping us evolve over the countless centuries to be better than we are.

Once safely back into our we decided to put ourselves into a self-imposed lock-down due to vastly spreading corona virus globally killing thousands of people. More than the losses here on the Earth, Karolla was very worried about her own home planet, until after three weeks Josh whose isolation had ended picked up a radio signal from outer space coming toward us with an update from her father.

In it there was news that the virus that had devastated his planet had died off naturally after only about six months giving us all hope of getting back to normal, but how wrong were we on Earth to be. Over the following year and beyond the lives of all where to be changed so many in many ways. As for Karolla, Ataya and I we are all well at this time, but very sad after finding out that our friend Mavis and three other residences of the care home we visited had died from COVID.

Author's Gallery Over the Years

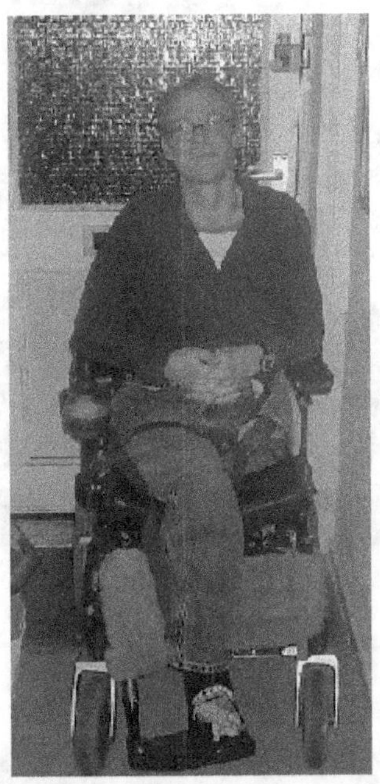

Figure 1. Home after first leg came off

Figure 2. Dressed up for Christmas 2011

Figure 3. Me in 2004

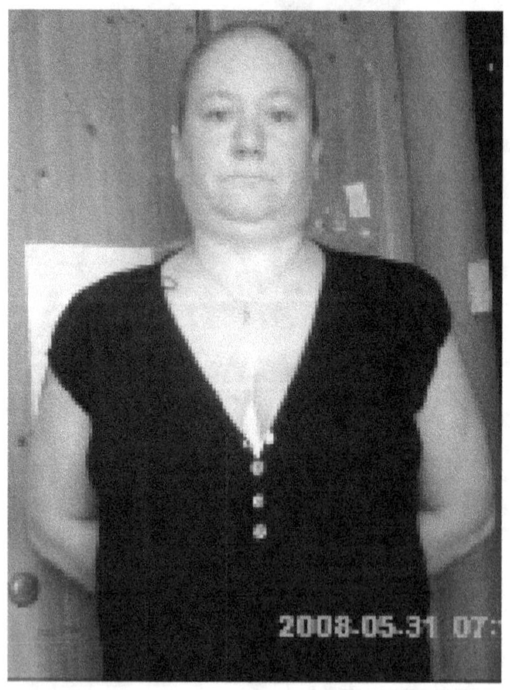

Figure 4. My Lovely Michelle 2007

Figure 5. Me with only one leg

Figure 6. My wife Michelle in 2003

Figure 7. Me posing for picture

Figure 8. My custom-built Trike

Figure 9. Wedding day in April 2003

Figure 10. After 3 months using cannabis

Figure 11. Granddaughter sleeps when grandad is there

Figure 12. Raising money for NABD national association of
bikers with disabilities

Figure 13. After 4 months using cannabis

Figure 14. Me in Year 2012 with my Awesome T-shirt Sign